PHINEAS L. MACGUIRE . . .

GETS COOKING!

For Win Hill and Gavin Schulz,
two of my favorite geniuses

The author would like to thank the most fabulous Caitlyn Dlouhy and the most marvelous Ariel Colletti for being utterly fabulous and marvelous, and she wants to give a big tip of the hat to Lyn Streck, science teacher extraordinaire. Thanks to Kaitlin Severini, pretty much the best copy editor ever, and to Sonia Chaghatzbanian, the most marvelous book designer. Thank you to the fantastic Laura Ferguson for all of her fantastic work, and lots of love and gratitude to the usual gang of family and friends who keep the author centered and sane, which is no easy job.

Also by Frances O'Roark Dowell

Chicken Boy • *Dovey Coe* • *Falling In* • *The Kind of Friends We Used to Be* • *Phineas L. MacGuire . . . Blasts Off!* • *Phineas L. MacGuire . . . Erupts!* • *Phineas L. MacGuire . . . Gets Slimed!* *The Second Life of Abigail Walker* • *The Secret Language of Girls* *Shooting the Moon* • *The Sound of Your Voice, Only Really Far Away* • *Ten Miles Past Normal* • *Where I'd Like to Be*

atheneum

ATHENEUM BOOKS FOR YOUNG READERS • An imprint of Simon & Schuster Children's Publishing Division • 1230 Avenue of the Americas, New York, New York 10020 • This book is a work of fiction. Any references to historical events, real people, or real places are used fictitiously. Other names, characters, places, and events are products of the author's imagination, and any resemblance to actual events or places or persons, living or dead, is entirely coincidental. For information about special discounts for bulk purchases, please contact Simon & Schuster Special Sales at 1-866-506-1949 or business@simonandschuster.com. • The Simon & Schuster Speakers Bureau can bring authors to your live event. For more information or to book an event, contact the Simon & Schuster Speakers Bureau at 1-866-248-3049 or visit our website at www.simonspeakers.com. • Book design by Sonia Chaghatzbanian • The text for this book is set in Garth Graphic. • The illustrations for this book are rendered in pencil. • Manufactured in the United States of America • 0913 OFF • First Edition • 10 9 8 7 6 5 4 3 2 1 • CIP data for this book is available from the Library of Congress • ISBN 978-1-4814-0294-1 • ISBN 978-1-4814-0101-2 (eBook)

FROM THE HIGHLY SCIENTIFIC NOTEBOOKS OF PHINEAS L. MACGUIRE

PHINEAS L. MACGUIRE . . .

GETS COOKING!

FLOUR

BUTTER

by FRANCES O'ROARK DOWELL

illustrated by PRESTON McDANIELS

atheneum

Atheneum Books for Young Readers

New York London Toronto Sydney New Delhi

Worms

My name is Phineas L. MacGuire.

A few people call me Phineas, but most people call me Mac. Yesterday, when I was riding the bus to school, I came up with a bunch of cool things the *L* in my name could stand for. My list included:

1. Lithosphere (the outmost shell of a rocky planet)
2. Lunar Eclipse

3. Light-Year
4. Labrador Whisperer

Unfortunately, the *L* in my name does not stand for any of those things. It stands for Listerman, which was, like, my mom's great-aunt Tulip's last name or something. My mom is very big on family traditions, but even she's not allowed to call me Listerman.

I mean, ever.

You can probably tell by the first three things on my list of *L* names that I am a scientist. In fact, I'm the best fourth-grade scientist at Woodbrook Elementary School. Or at least sort of the best. There's this girl in my class named Aretha who might be kind of as good at science as I am, but her goal is not to be the greatest scientist in the whole world one day, which mine is. I think that gives me the edge.

The last thing on my list has to do with a certain Labrador retriever named Lemon Drop. I walk Lemon Drop every day after school, and earlier this year I did a major dog slobber experiment inspired by Lemon Drop's natural dog slobberiness. It was awesome.

The fourth grade has been my best year as a scientist ever. So far I have:

1. Gotten an honorable mention in the fourth-grade science fair.
2. Grown my own slime and established the Phineas L. MacGuire Mold Museum in my bedroom.
3. Performed important dog slobber experiments that prove, when you get down to it, that slobber is alive.
4. Attended Space Camp and ridden the Mars roller coaster without throwing up.

For most people, that would be enough for one year, but

when you're a scientist like me, you want to do scientific stuff all the time.

The problem is, sometimes you run out of good ideas.

I've been in the middle of a serious dry spell that has lasted over two weeks, and I've been feeling pretty grumpy about it. Usually I'm in a good mood, so people notice when I'm not. Yesterday my teacher, Mrs. Tuttle, put one of the rubber frogs from the jar she keeps on her desk on top of my head. She was trying to make me laugh.

Everybody else laughed, but I didn't.

At lunch my best friend, Ben Robbins, who is a genius artist, drew a bunch of pictures of me as a superhero scientist. There was one where I was wearing a lab coat and holding up an exploding beaker of chemicals. It was really cool-looking, but it didn't cheer me up.

During recess Aretha Timmons went out and found three dried worms to give me for my dried worm collection. This should have made me extremely happy, since this hasn't been a good spring for dried worms, and I'm behind on my monthly quota. And it sort of did make me happy, but only for about ten minutes.

Then I went back to feeling grumpy because I didn't have a good science project to do.

My mom has been grumpy a lot lately too. She's a naturally irritable person, but that's not the same thing as being grumpy. Being irritated is a reaction to a situation. Being grumpy is a state of mind.

"I don't know why I can't lose this last five pounds," she complained at dinner last night. She took another bite of pizza before saying, "Phyllis and I walk two miles every day on our lunch break. You'd think the pounds would just fall off."

My stepdad, Lyle, reached across the table and grabbed a slice from the box. "You look great, Liz. I'm glad you're exercising, but you don't need to do it to lose weight."

"We could stop eating pizza all the time," I said. "That might help."

I should point out that I wasn't actually eating pizza. Pizza is pretty much my favorite food group, but I've learned you can get tired of even stuff you love a lot if you have to eat it three nights a week. So for the second night in a row I was eating a bowl of Cheerios® for dinner.

My mom's expression was 50 percent grumpy and 50 percent irritated. "Mac, we've been through this. I'm tired when I get home after a long day at work. So's Lyle. Cooking takes time, and it takes energy, two things I really don't have a lot of at the end of the day."

I shrugged. "I'm just saying that scientifically speaking, it's hard to lose weight when all you eat is pizza. I'm not complaining or anything."

"You might be complaining just a little bit, and I guess I don't blame you," my mom said, and then she smiled a grumpy sort of smile. "I can't tell you how often I wished the workday was like a school day—you know, home by three, plenty of time to get everything done. If I got home at three every day, I'd be able to—"

She paused. She looked at me for what seemed like a really long time. And then she got this smile on her face. A very scary kind of smile.

"I know just what to do about it," my mom said, picking up her phone and tapping on the keyboard. After she was done, she said, "There! Problem solved!"

Lyle and I looked at each other like, *What's going on?*

My mom lost her grumpy expression. In fact, she looked downright happy. That sort of scared me, if you want to know the truth.

"I've just texted Sarah that tomorrow when you get home from school, she's to take you to the grocery store."

By Sarah, she means my babysitter from outer space. Going anywhere with Sarah was

not high on my list of things to do.

"Why?" I asked.

My mom smiled. "Because from now on, you're going to cook dinner, Mac. And I know you'll do an amazing job."

"Wait, you have to do all the cooking from now on?" Ben shook his head, then swung his way across the monkey bars. "That's, like, a mega amount of work, Mac," he said when he reached the other side. "You won't have time to do anything else."

"I just have to make dinner," I told him. "Lyle's still going to make our lunches, and we're all sort of on our own for breakfast."

"Even Margaret?"

Margaret is my two-year-old sister. "No, my mom fixes her breakfast. Only Margaret never eats it. She just mushes up the toast and the banana and smears it all over her face."

Ben grimaced. "Little kids are so gross."

"It's actually sort of cool-looking," I told him, grabbing onto the first bar of the monkey bars and swinging back and forth. "Like slime mold."

As far as I'm concerned, there is nothing cooler in the world than a little bit of slime.

"But I don't get how you're going to do dinner all by yourself," Ben said, starting to draw a picture in the dirt with a stick. "You're not even ten yet. That's kinda young to be in charge of the most important meal of the day."

"I thought breakfast was the most important meal of the day."

"Yeah, that's what Mrs. Tuttle says, but here's my question: Do you have dessert with breakfast?"

I shook my head.

"I rest my case," Ben said, taking a bow. "You can have dessert with lunch, it's true, but usually it's a pretty small dessert, like a couple of cookies or something. But dessert after dinner? We're talking ice cream, my friend, we're talking cake, pie, baked Alaska."

"You have baked Alaska for dessert?"

"Theoretically speaking, I could," Ben said. "I'm not actually sure what baked Alaska is, to be honest, but I know nobody ever has it after they've eaten breakfast."

I didn't know anybody who ate dessert after breakfast, though I did know a few people who sort of ate dessert *for* breakfast. There's this kid in our class, Roland Forth, who gets on the bus every morning carrying a doughnut wrapped in a napkin. Some days it's a powdered doughnut, other days it's one with sprinkles. Everybody around him says, "Hey, Roland, I'll be your best friend if you give me half," or "Hey, Roland, if you give me your doughnut, I'll do your homework," but Roland never shares. He just sits and eats and makes these little happy humming noises.

Roland Forth is a famous hummer, in case you were wondering. It's like having a radio playing in your class all day long.

In case you're wondering, Roland Forth is also pretty annoying.

I sat down next to Ben in the dirt and started collecting pebbles to make a frame for the picture he was drawing. "My mom thinks making me cook dinner is the greatest idea in the world, but it's pretty stupid, if you ask me. First of all, I don't know anything about cooking. I mean, okay, I can use the toaster oven to heat up frozen waffles, but that's it. And when I told my mom I don't know how to cook, she said that Sarah can teach me."

Ben's eyes widened. "Whoa! That's harsh."

Totally harsh. Time with Sarah is not time well spent, in my book. She is seriously into purple, a color I happen to be allergic to, and she is always trying to make me eat nutritious snacks after school. I would find her 100 percent annoying except for the fact that she built a mold museum in my room earlier this year and found twelve dried worms for my collection.

You have to admit, it's hard to be 100 percent annoyed by a babysitter who understands your passion for mold.

Still, spending my afternoons cooking with Sarah did not sound like a great plan to me. It sounded more like a punishment.

"And anyway," I told Ben, "cooking seems totally boring. Besides, it's really more of a girl thing than a boy thing."

"Excuse me, did I just hear you say cooking is a girl thing?"

I looked up to see Aretha Timmons standing behind me. Uh-oh. Aretha definitely didn't like it when you said only boys can do this and only girls can do that. Come to think of it, Ben didn't either, since he wanted to be an artist and his dad said that art was for girls.

"Well, you know," I stammered, "it just seems like something girls, uh, sort of like more than boys. I mean, Melissa Beamer and Michelle Lee are always talking about baking cupcakes, and Stacey Windham watches every show on the Cooking Channel."

Aretha put her hands on her hips. "And you think that means cooking is a girl thing? Just because you know three girls who cook? Well, I can name at least three guys who cook, number one being my dad. He cooks dinner every night."

Come to think of it, my dad cooks a lot too. I go stay with him every other weekend, and he makes these big pans of lasagna and baked ziti. In fact, he's a much better cook than my mom, except when it comes to pumpkin pie. My mom is, like, the world's best pumpkin pie maker. It's one of her most stellar qualities, besides the fact she totally gets that I'm a serious scientist, which not every mom of a fourth grader would.

Aretha raised three fingers. She tapped one and said, "Okay, so number one guy cook is my dad, and"—she tapped another finger—"number two is my grandfather, who taught my dad to cook in the first place. Number three is Mr. Reid. You know those awesome chocolate chip cookies at the bake sales? Mr. Reid!"

Mr. Reid is our school janitor and a fellow scientist. I didn't know he was a baker too. "I thought Mrs. Reid made those cookies," I said.

Aretha shook her head. "Mac, Mac, Mac. Welcome to the twenty-first century. *Everybody* cooks. Besides, I thought you'd be into cooking."

I stood up and wiped the dirt from my jeans. "Why?!"

"Because cooking is science," Aretha said. "It's chemistry!"

Ben drew a huge atomic cloud in the dirt. "Even I knew that!" he said.

Chemistry? I thought about scientists in lab coats wearing protective goggles and gloves and pouring dangerous chemical concoctions into beakers, watching as purple-and-blue smoke poured out. I thought about the chemistry set my mom wouldn't let me get because she thought I'd burn a huge hole in the kitchen floor with the chemicals.

When I thought about chemistry, I never once thought about cooking.

But now I could sort of see it.

"I need to go do some research," I told Aretha and Ben. "When's recess over?"

Aretha checked her totally awesome watch, which doesn't just tell the time, it gives you the weather report too. "Ten minutes," she informed me.

That was just enough time to get started. I ran to the library and got permission from Mrs. Rosen, our school librarian, to use the computer. I searched "chemicals used in cooking," and this is the list I made:

1. Baking soda, also known as $NaHCO_3$ or sodium bicarbonate

2. Salt, also known as NaCl or sodium chloride
3. Baking powder, a mix of cream of tartar and sodium bicarbonate
4. Cream of tartar, which is potassium bitartrate, also called potassium hydrogen tartrate
5. Lemon juice, also known as citric acid, also known as $C_6H_8O_7$

Here's what else I discovered. There's a kind of science that's all about experimenting with chemistry in cooking. You can go to college to study it, and even get your PhD.

In other words, I wouldn't just be a cook; I'd be a molecular gastronomist.

That, I liked the sound of.

Going to the grocery store with Sarah Fortemeyer is not my idea of fun. In fact, I try to avoid doing anything with Sarah if at all possible. My Sarah Fortemeyer phobia started last year, when she first started babysitting us and asked if she could paint my fingernails. She was testing out different colors, and she'd already painted her nails and Margaret's.

I'd run upstairs as fast as I could and shoved a chair against my door. Ever since then I've avoided Sarah Fortemeyer like two weeks' worth of extra homework whenever possible.

But today she wasn't so bad. First of all, she wasn't armed with fingernail polish. Then, she actually let me do the shopping by myself while she and Margaret looked at magazines. "Pasta's on aisle two, and so is the spaghetti sauce," she told me, handing me the list. "Your mom says to get the organic kind. Frozen garlic bread's in the frozen food section, and the bagged salad is over in produce."

I have to admit, it didn't sound like the most scientific dinner in the world. Where was the baking soda? The citric acid? Tonight's dinner was strictly amateur stuff. Normally this would be okay, since I'm a kid, but I'm also a scientist.

As a scientist, I was hoping for the kind of dinner that might blow up at the last minute.

I pushed the cart to aisle two. Was there a science to cooking spaghetti? I wondered. Why did the water need to be boiling to cook pasta?

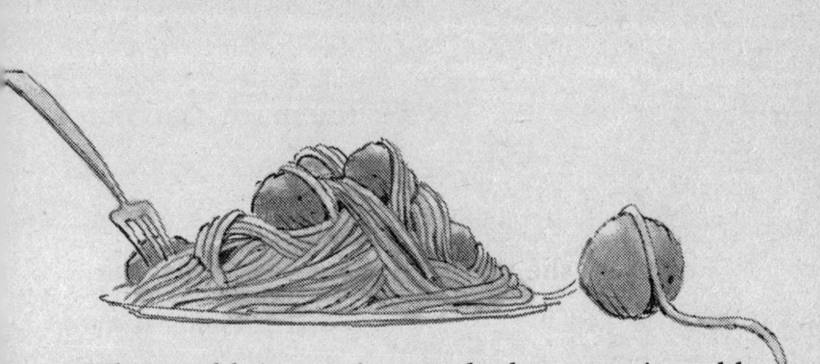

Why couldn't you just soak the pasta in cold water? Would it still get soft?

When I got to the shelves where all the pasta was, I could see it wasn't going to be as simple as just grabbing a box and chucking it into the cart. If my calculations were correct, there were seventeen different kinds of spaghetti, including thin spaghetti, regular spaghetti, whole wheat spaghetti, pasta-plus spaghetti, and extra-long spaghetti. There were a bunch of different brands, too. I decided to get the box that looked most familiar, but I got the extra-large size, because I wasn't sure how much spaghetti I needed to cook for four people. I read the instructions on the back of the box, which said a serving was four ounces, but that didn't seem like enough to me. Besides, better too much than not enough, right?

There were even more kinds of spaghetti sauce than spaghetti, but there were only two kinds of organic sauce, which made choosing a lot easier. I got the kind that cost eight dollars instead of the kind that cost four dollars, because I figured the eight-dollar stuff would be twice as good.

"Wow, pretty fancy," Sarah said when I showed her everything I'd gotten. "Are you sure your mom wants you to spend that much on the sauce?"

"She only wants the best for her family," I assured Sarah.

"Okay," Sarah said with a shrug. "Let's get this stuff home and start cooking."

When I walked into the kitchen, I decided to think of it as my lab. The stove was a giant

Bunsen burner, and the pots and pans were beakers and flasks. *If only I had a lab coat,* I thought, and then I had a brilliant idea. I ran upstairs and grabbed one of Lyle's white work shirts. It was long enough on me to look like a coat. All I had to do was roll up the sleeves a million times and I looked like a genius scientist.

If I did say so myself.

Next, I needed a plan. When you work in a lab, you have to be organized. I read the instructions on the pasta box, which said that I should boil the spaghetti for ten to twelve minutes. I started to write that down on the notepad my mom leaves on the counter, but then I stopped. Ten minutes didn't seem long enough for two pounds of pasta. I checked out the serving size, which was four ounces. If you multiply four ounces by four servings, you get sixteen ounces, or a pound. But since I was going to make two pounds of spaghetti so we could have leftovers the next night, I calculated I should boil the pasta for twice as long: twenty to twenty-four minutes.

Easy peasy.

I got out a big pot from the cabinet, filled it up with water, and then put it on the burner. Here's where I ran into my first problem.

I'm not allowed to use the stove.

"Hey, Sarah!" I called. "How am I supposed to cook dinner if turning on the stove is against the rules?"

Sarah came in from the living room, where she'd been having a tea party with Margaret. "Do you know how to turn it on?"

I felt my face turn red. "Uh, not really."

"No need to be embarrassed, little buddy," Sarah said, patting me on the shoulder, which made me feel even more embarrassed. "There's a first time for everything."

Then she showed me what I needed to do. We have a gas stove, which is pretty cool, because you have to get the gas going and then twist the knob to just the right place. *Swoosh!*

A flame pops up and you're ready to cook!

The instructions on the pasta box said I had to let the water come to a boil before I put the spaghetti in the pot. I didn't know how long that would take, so I thought I'd go ahead and pour the sauce into another pan and start heating

that up. Which is where I ran into my second problem.

I couldn't get the lid off the jar.

"Like I said, there's a first time for everything, right?" Sarah said, patting me on the back again. "The trick to this is use a rubber glove. It gives you more traction, which, in case you're wondering, is just another word for adhesive force."

I hadn't been wondering, actually, but it was good to know.

Sarah wrapped the lid with one of the yellow rubber gloves by the sink, took a deep breath, and twisted. The top popped off.

"Know why the jar makes that popping sound when it comes off?" Sarah asked.

"Um, I'm not sure," I said, my face getting even redder. I was starting to feel like a total failurezoid in the lab. "Maybe it's gas that's being released from the jar? Maybe the contents are under pressure, and then you open the lid and everything rushes out?"

Sarah nodded. "That sounds like a good

explanation. Hey, do you know how to turn on the oven? You need to start preheating it for the garlic bread."

That, I did know.

Five minutes later I had the sauce heating up in a pot, the garlic bread unwrapped and on a baking tray, and the box of spaghetti ready to dump in the water, just as soon as the water started to boil.

I also had six spaghetti sauce stains on Lyle's shirt, but I was pretty sure they'd wash out.

Then a couple of things happened all at once. One, my mom got home from work. Two, Sarah started giving her the daily report. Three, the water came to a boiling point, which means, in case you're wondering, that it had reached a temperature of 212 degrees.

So while my mom and Sarah were talking, I dumped the spaghetti into the pot. All two pounds of it.

That might not have been the greatest idea in the world.

After dinner was over, I decided to write a lab report, which is what scientists do, whether their experiments are successful or not. I wrote down the name of the experiment, the steps

I had taken, and the results. Finally, I wrote down a list of everything I'd learned, including:

1. After you put spaghetti in boiling water, you need to stir it. Otherwise, it all clumps together into one big pasta log.
2. It's also a good idea to stir your spaghetti sauce if you don't want most of it to burn to the bottom of the pot.
3. Two pounds of pasta is enough to feed a family of four for about a week.
4. When you cook pasta for twenty minutes, it sort of disintegrates. Forget about eating it. I mean, just totally forget about it.
5. Cheerios for dinner is really pretty good, especially with garlic bread.

I spent lunch today reading this book my mom gave me called *The Joy of Cooking.* After last night's dinner disaster, I thought I'd be kicked off kitchen duty, but my mom says every cook makes mistakes, especially at the beginning, and the only way to learn is to try, try again.

Actually, my mom was pretty nice about me ruining dinner. The only thing that made her mad was me wearing Lyle's shirt. She was a little bit irritated because I got spaghetti sauce on it, and slightly more irritated that I'd spent eight bucks on the sauce in the first place, but she was super mad because wearing oversize clothing—especially a big shirt with long sleeves—in the kitchen is dangerous.

"Safety in the lab is a scientist's number one priority," she told me. "So tomorrow night, wear a T-shirt."

At lunch, I was reading the chapter called "Know Your Ingredients" when Ben practically skidded into the chair next to me.

"Fantastizoid news, Mac!" he exclaimed, smacking a piece of paper on top of my book. "Your great cooking experiment could not come at a better time! Just look at this contest we're going to win!"

I glanced at the piece of paper, which looked like it had been torn out of a magazine. THE COOKING CHANNEL'S FIRST ANNUAL RECIPE CONTEST! the headline shouted up at me in superbright yellow letters. ENTER AND WIN $10,000, PLUS A BRAND NEW KITCHEN!

"What do I need a brand-new kitchen for?" I asked, pushing the announcement back toward Ben. "I've already got a kitchen."

Ben shook his head. "It's not the kitchen we're after, Mac. It's the money! Ten thousand buckaroos! We'll split it fifty-fifty and each still have a load of dough. Me, I'm using my half to go to Hawaii and learn how to surf."

Ben's big dream has always been to be a rock star surfboarder. Well, his *big* big dream is to be a famous cartoonist, and he thinks surfing is a part of the cartoonist lifestyle.

I have no idea where he comes up with this stuff.

"Okay, so the money would be nice," I said. "The only problem is, I'm just learning how to cook, and you don't know how to cook at all. So how are we supposed to come up with some award-winning recipe?"

"We'll spend this weekend having a Cooking Channel marathon at my apartment," Ben said, sounding confident. "We'll pick up all sorts of useful information, some good cooking tips and what have you, and by Sunday we'll figure out a great recipe. According to the announcement, we have to e-mail our recipe, preferably with pix of the finished product, by Monday, April 8. That gives us two and a half weeks."

Suddenly there was a loud popping noise to my left. I turned and saw Aretha popping her pencil against the table. At our school, fourth-grade boys and girls don't sit together at lunch, even when they're fellow scientists. If you do, people will automatically start calling you boyfriend and girlfriend.

I try to avoid that at all costs, and so does Aretha. So what we usually do at lunch is sit at tables next to each other, in case we have any important scientific information to share.

Aretha had her *Girl Scout Handbook* open in front of her, but she was looking straight at me. "Two weeks isn't much time, Mac. The good news is you're in luck. I've just started working on a cooking badge, and helping you would help me."

"But I don't really know how to cook," I repeated. "I think it would help to know how to actually cook stuff if I wanted to make up my own recipe."

"Yeah, which is where my great idea comes in,"

Aretha said. "See, I've got to do this unit on eggs to get my badge. My dad's going to teach me how to cook eggs on Saturday, and it would be a lot more fun if you and Ben were there. I bet my dad would give us all kinds of helpful cooking hints. Plus, I've got to make up an egg recipe and come up with a food science project. So we can brainstorm together. Three brains are better than one." She glanced at Ben. "Or two brains. Whatever."

Aretha started packing up her lunch bag. "The thing about coming up with recipes is, you don't have to be totally original. Think of something you really love to eat, and then imagine ways you could make it better."

"Right!" Ben exclaimed. "Like me, personally, I love a banana-peanut-butter smoothie. And you know what would make that even more better? Bacon. See! I'm a genius! We've got this contest in the bag."

"You think you're going to win with a banana-peanut-butter-and-bacon smoothie?" I asked.

"You think I should throw some strawberry jelly in there too?"

Aretha and I looked at each other. Then we looked at Ben.

Then we both yelled "No!" so loud that everybody in the cafeteria turned around and looked at us.

Ben shrugged. "It was just an idea."

"So what are you going to cook for dinner tonight, Mac?" Aretha asked, closing her *Girl Scout Handbook*. It was almost time to go out to the playground for recess.

"My mom said maybe I should try something simple, like homemade waffles. Which would be good, since we've got all the ingredients."

"I love breakfast for dinner!" Ben said. "As long as you still get real dessert, that is."

I lugged *The Joy of Cooking* out with me

to the playground. I was pretending it was a chemistry textbook, which it sort of was, although it probably had more oatmeal cookie recipes than your average chemistry textbook. While Ben went to play soccer with a bunch of third graders, I sat down on the stairs by the door and got back to reading about ingredients.

It was actually a lot more interesting than you might think.

For instance, I learned that yeast cells reproduce really fast if you give them some warm water and sugar. It turns out that water and sugar are to yeast what chocolate chip ice cream is to human beings.

While the cells are growing and reproducing, they produce these things called enzymes. When I looked it up in the dictionary later, I learned that enzymes are catalysts for chemical reactions. In other words, enzymes are the movers and shakers of the chemical world. The enzymes produced by the yeast convert starch into sugar. The yeast eats the sugar and then produces carbon dioxide gas, and that's what makes the dough get all puffy.

To put it another way, it's kind of like the yeast ate a bunch of junk food and farted.

But in a good way.

I was just starting to get into the section on baking powder and biscuits when a shadow fell over the page. I looked up and saw Evan Forbes. As always, he was wearing red Chucks, a gray hoodie, and a blue-and-red-striped T-shirt. It was sort of his uniform. He kicked up some

dust with one of his Chucks and sneered at me.

I knew that whatever happened next, it would not be good.

I've never understood kids like Evan Forbes. For one thing, it seems like he lives to make other kids unhappy. For another thing, he never does his homework. Just today, Mrs. Tuttle dismissed us for lunch but told Evan to wait. I was the last one out of the classroom, so I overheard her say, "I'm going to have to call your parents, Evan. This is the third time this week you haven't turned in your math assignment."

"Go ahead," Evan had answered in a loud voice, like he didn't care if anybody heard. "My parents say it's my choice. If I don't feel like doing homework, I don't have to."

Yeah, right, I thought. I glanced back over my shoulder, expecting to see Evan looking all tough and mean, but to my surprise he sort of looked like he was about to cry.

It was pretty weird, if you want to know the truth.

"Hey, Mr. Top Chef!" Evan said, reaching down and flipping my book shut. "I thought you were some hotshot scientist or something, but I guess I was wrong about that. It turns out you're a culinary artist!"

Actually, I was kind of impressed by Evan's vocabulary. "Culinary" was a pretty advanced word for a Neanderthal like him.

"I *am* a scientist," I told him. "Have you ever heard of something called a molecular gastronomist?"

"I've heard of a chowderhead," Evan said. "That's what you look like to me."

"I don't know how to make chowder yet," I said. I was trying to make a joke, but my voice came out sort of squeaky. "Besides, I think I might be allergic to clams. I'm allergic to a lot of stuff."

Have I mentioned that I'm allergic to fifteen things, including avocados, cottage cheese, grape jelly, celery, and anything purple? My mom says that the only things I'm actually

allergic to are peanuts and cat hair, but I have documented proof that purple ink gives me hives.

Evan shook his head. "I oughta clobber you. But listen, I'm gonna give you a break. My sources tell me you're all into this cooking thing now, and I could really use some brownies. My mom's on this health kick, and sugar's, like, against the law in my house. I haven't had a brownie in two weeks. So here's the deal—you make me some brownies, and I'll let you live a little while longer."

"Why don't you just go to the store and buy some brownies?" I asked.

Evan shook his head. "Store-bought brownies aren't the same as homemade. Not even in the same universe. So meet me here tomorrow before school with a dozen brownies in an unmarked paper bag. That is, if you're interested in keeping all of your teeth."

I watched Evan walk across the playground and join a game of football. It was supposed to be touch football, but every time the playground monitor turned her back, somebody got tackled. I mean, tackled as in thrown down to the ground and trampled on.

Scientifically speaking, I was in big trouble.

There were a few minutes left in recess, so I ran down to Mr. Reid's office. Maybe he could give me some helpful hints for baking brownies.

"The best recipe I know is in that book you're holding right there," Mr. Reid told me. "Let's take a look, and I'll walk you through it."

Mr. Reid pulled up a chair next to his desk, and we both sat down. "So when do you want to make these brownies?" he asked, searching the

The Joy of Cooking's index for the recipe.

"As soon as possible," I told him. I didn't mention that my life might depend on it. "The minute I get home from school."

"Do you know if you've got what you need?" He found the brownie recipe page and ran his finger down the list of ingredients. "Do you have butter and eggs?"

I nodded.

"Flour and sugar?"

I nodded again.

"Four ounces of unsweetened baking chocolate?"

This time I shook my head. "I'm pretty sure we have chocolate chips. Could I just use those?"

"Nope, because the recipe already has sugar in it, you see. But no worries—I always keep a few baking supplies in my drawer here." Mr. Reid pulled out his bottom desk drawer, and I could see that he wasn't kidding. There were plastic containers marked FLOUR and SUGAR and boxes of salt, baking powder, and baking soda. At the very back of the drawer was a box labeled BAKING CHOCOLATE.

"Sometimes, if one of the teachers is having a bad day, I take my ingredients up to the kitchen and bake 'em something. I'm pretty famous around here for my brownies, as a matter of fact."

Mr. Reid shook four little blocks of chocolate wrapped in wax paper out of the box and handed them to me. "Now, the tricky thing about chocolate is that it burns really easily when you melt it. So what you have to do is chop it up and put it in a microwave-safe bowl with the butter, which you need to cut up into cubes. Microwave it for forty-five seconds, stir, and microwave it again—but only for forty-five seconds. Let it sit a minute, then microwave it for maybe thirty seconds."

"Why does chocolate burn so easily?"

"Low melting temperature," Mr. Reid explained. "It melts in your mouth, right? So let's say it melts at ninety degrees. Heat it up much higher than that, the cocoa butter separates from the solids and everything burns up. It's not pretty."

"I wonder why things have different melting points," I said. "I mean, all liquids have the same boiling point, right? And everything freezes at the same point, when they get below thirty-two degrees."

"Actually, Mac, only water freezes at thirty-two degrees," Mr. Reid told me. "Everything has its own freezing point, which is usually the same as its melting point. It just depends on whether something's moving toward the state of becoming a solid or becoming a liquid."

I must have looked as confused as I felt,

because Mr. Reid smiled and said, "Just think about a piece of ice, Mac. Ice is frozen water. Freezes at thirty-two degrees Fahrenheit, right? So when does that piece of ice start to melt?"

I thought about it for a minute and then made a guess. "Eighty degrees?"

Mr. Reid shook his head. "Way too high, Mac. Now, this might twist your brain into a knot, but the melting point of ice and the freezing point of ice are exactly the same. It's called being in equilibrium. So water freezes at thirty-two degrees, but ice can be considered to be melting at thirty-two degrees. If chocolate melts at ninety degrees, it also is starting to freeze at ninety degrees."

You know the weird thing? I almost understood what Mr. Reid was saying.

Almost.

But not really.

"Okay, enough

about thermodynamics," Mr. Reid said, looking at his watch. "You should be back in your classroom. Do you have any more questions about brownies? You can always call me at home later. Just follow the instructions, Mac. Cooking is chemistry, right?"

"Right." I nodded, trying to look confident. All I knew for sure was that if I burned the chocolate, I couldn't make the brownies, and if I didn't make brownies, I was a goner.

When Ben heard I was making brownies, he immediately wanted to help. "This could be like practice for when we come up with our prizewinning recipe. We could mix stuff in the brownie batter—you know, experiment. We could mix in bacon!"

"You're obsessed with bacon," I told him. "Bacon in brownies, bacon in milk shakes. Bacon's not even healthy."

"My mom says that nitrate-free bacon isn't so bad." Ben lowered his voice to a whisper, since Mrs. Tuttle was giving us the evil eye for talking during silent reading period. "The fact is, Mac, bacon just makes everything better. That's sort of my motto."

"Well, I'm not putting bacon in these brownies," I whispered back. "And I'm—I'm not allowed to have anyone over today. You know, since I messed up Lyle's shirt and everything."

"Bummer," Ben whispered. "Maybe tomorrow?"

"Maybe," I said, and then I pointed to the book on my desk, like we better start reading before Mrs. Tuttle got really mad and started throwing frogs at us.

I hated lying to Ben about not being able to come over, but I knew if he helped me make the brownies, he'd end up eating at least half of them, and then Evan Forbes would half-way kill me. Which maybe was better than being all the way killed, but not much.

When I got home, Sarah and Margaret were playing beauty parlor in the kitchen. "Hey, Mac, have a snack attack!" Sarah called out when I walked in. "There's some yogurt in the fridge."

"I'm allergic to yogurt," I reminded her, dropping my backpack by the door. "All flavors."

"Your mom says you're not," Sarah said, smearing some raspberry-colored lipstick on Margaret's lips. "And she says you need more protein in your diet. Yogurt's perfect."

"Except for the fact that I'd probably go into anaphylactic shock the minute I ate some," I told her.

"That's what happens with peanuts, Mac. Not yogurt."

"Anyway, I don't

have time for a snack," I said. "I need to get cooking. I've got brownies to make."

Margaret clapped her hands. "Brownies! Yum!"

"Sorry, Margaret, they're for school. I'll make you some tomorrow."

"Wow, you're really getting into this baking thing, huh?" Sarah pulled Margaret toward her so she could put red stuff on her cheeks. "It makes sense, I guess."

"Why? Because cooking is chemistry, and I'm a scientist?"

Sarah smiled. "That, plus chicks dig a guy who bakes."

I could feel the hives popping up across my back. Have I mentioned that I'm allergic to girls, too?

Well, I am.

I was super careful to follow the recipe. All I had was the chocolate that Mr. Reid gave me, so I couldn't mess up. I chopped up the chocolate and put it in a microwave-safe bowl with the butter, and I did exactly what Mr. Reid had told me to. To my majorzoid happiness, the chocolate melted without burning.

And it smelled better than anything in the world.

How did it taste before I mixed in the sugar?

You don't want to know.

Neither my mom nor Lyle do much baking, so I wasn't prepared for the amazing smells that came out of the oven. In fact, they smelled so good, I had to call my dad and tell him about them.

"Best smell in the world," he agreed. I could hear his team behind him, yelling and joking around. My dad teaches high school math and coaches the Mathlete team after school. "In fact, when you're here next weekend, let's make some."

"I'll be an expert by then," I told him. "And this weekend I'm going over to Aretha's to make eggs. She's working on a cooking badge for Girl Scouts."

"Great! You can make omelets for breakfast!" A loud burst of noise erupted through the phone.

"Whoops, gotta run—we've got a totally out-of-control quadratic equation situation going on here."

I hung up the phone and breathed in some more of that great brownie smell. When the timer went off, I pulled the brownies out of the oven. They looked perfect. They smelled perfect.

And okay, they tasted perfect too.

I mean, I couldn't give Evan Forbes brownies that hadn't been through a taste test, could I?

The only problem was, after the brownies were done, I still had to clean the kitchen. I looked at my watch—it was five fifteen. By the time the kitchen was clean it was almost six, and I hadn't even thought about starting dinner.

I guess it's a good thing everyone in my family likes Cheerios, huh?

PHINEAS, ARETHA, AND BEN are determined to create the kookiest, yummiest dessert ever for the bake-off. All they need are some cooking tips from Aretha's dad, and maybe a little bit of bacon, to perfect their brownie recipe. Phineas's cooking assignment is going great so far, and he's learning a ton about ingredients—such as what makes pancakes fluffy—but Evan Forbes is still demanding a fresh batch of brownies every day before school. Can Phineas figure out a scheme to end Evan's hunger streak without ending up getting clobbered, or in detention?

FIND OUT IN THE NEXT INSTALLMENT OF

PHINEAS L. MACGUIRE . . .

GETS COOKING!

PART TWO: BROWNIES SOOTHE THE SAVAGE BEAST

FRANCES O'ROARK DOWELL is the bestselling and critically acclaimed author of *Dovey Coe*, *The Second Life of Abigail Walker*, *Chicken Boy*, *Falling In*, *Where I'd Like to Be*, *The Secret Language of Girls*, and of course, the Phineas L. MacGuire series. She lives with her husband and two sons in Durham, North Carolina.

Connect with Frances online at FrancesDowell.com.